For Mary Ballard

B.W.

A GOLDEN BOOK · NEW YORK

Western Publishing Company, Inc., Racine, Wisconsin 53404

Library of Congress Catalog Card Number: 92-70398
ISBN: 0-307-17874-9/ISBN: 0-307-62874-1 (lib. bdg.)   A MCMXCIII

THE BIG GOLDEN BOOK OF

Knights and Castles

By Barbara Weisberg
Illustrated by Gino D'Achille

CONTENTS

DANGEROUS TIMES

wo thousand years ago the city of Rome ruled a mighty empire. Rome was a center of learning, art, government, and trade for all those who lived in the lands around the Mediterranean Sea.

Beyond the city, throughout Rome's territory, there were bustling towns filled with fine homes and busy shops. Well-traveled sea routes linked Rome to faraway places in Asia and Africa. Education was valued, and compared to earlier times, more people knew how to read and write. The Roman people lived by a strong code of laws, and crimes were punished.

By the 300s Rome ruled most of Europe, the northern coast of Africa, Egypt, and parts of the Middle East. But over time the Roman Empire became weak. A terrible plague spread sickness everywhere. Droughts ruined the farms and pastureland. Animals could not graze, and farmers could not grow as much food as people needed. Emperors governed harshly, and their unhappy subjects rebelled.

As Roman rulers tried to keep order, invaders swept down from northern Europe and Asia. Wave after wave of fierce intruders attacked Roman towns and villages. The Huns—led by their ruthless chief, Attila—the Visigoths, the Vandals, the Franks, and the Saxons attacked the Roman Empire, from the land we now call Spain all the way to Greece. In 455 the Vandals attacked the city of Rome. They burned and looted buildings. They stole the bronze roof from the Capitol building because they believed it was made of gold.

Soon Rome's achievements melted away until almost nothing was left. The vast system of roads was destroyed. Cities crumbled into ruins. Fewer and fewer people learned how to read and write. The Roman government and its laws no longer existed. Gangs of thieves roamed the countryside, and ordinary people lived in fear, without strong leaders to protect them.

This is what much of Europe was like at the beginning of the Middle Ages—the centuries between the fall of the Roman Empire, in the 400s, and the dawn of the modern era, in the 1500s.

When the Vandals invaded Rome in 455, they burned buildings and robbed the city of its treasures.

LORDS AND LOYAL KNIGHTS

he terror and lawlessness of the early Middle Ages did not last forever. Strong leaders slowly began to emerge. Often they were the sons and grandsons of the invaders who had helped destroy Rome. Through raids and theft, these men gained land and power. Their followers called these leaders "lords."

By the 700s there were many lords throughout Europe. Each one had to be ready to fight his enemies in order to protect his land and possessions. The homes of lords became fortresses, places that protected the lord and his followers. Called "castles," which comes from a Latin word meaning "fort," these huge buildings had thick walls, high towers, and dark, cold dungeons.

Ordinary men and women lived near the castle of their local lord on land he owned. In return for their hard work, the lord protected them. Mostly farmers, these people were called "serfs." Serfs were not allowed to move away from the lord's land. Often they were the descendants of people who had been conquered long ago.

A wealthy lord usually had a group of knights, who were highly skilled soldiers, living in the castle household. A knight promised to defend his lord's castle and lands and to attack his lord's enemies. A knight could be rewarded with land and a castle for his loyal service and, therefore, become a lord.

The strongest lord in a region gave land to less important lords. In return for land, they promised to help him in battle. The most powerful lords in Europe became known as "kings."

This new order of leadership was called "feudalism." Feudalism spread throughout Europe between the 1000s and the 1400s.

In feudal Europe the Christian faith created a bond between kings, lords, and serfs. Most people belonged to the Christian Church. Religious ceremonies marked their births, marriages, and deaths. Places called "monasteries," where religious men studied, became centers of learning.

Villages where ordinary people lived and worked were built on the lord's land and located close to the castle for protection.

WITHIN THE CASTLE WALLS

A castle was a little world all to itself. Many people lived and worked within a castle's walls. If the castle was attacked, those who lived inside could find everything they needed to survive. The castle was the home of the lord, his lady (which is what his wife and all women of high rank were called), their children, and their servants. Lords and knights from far and wide visited often and stayed for many weeks. Traveling singers, acrobats, jugglers, and poets also came and went, making mealtimes festive with merry songs and lively entertainment.

A wealthy lord might have as many as 100 servants and others working in the castle. There were women who did the castle's spinning, weaving, sewing, and embroidery. There were special servants who kept track of the large food supply. Cooks and bakers prepared the enormous dinners of meat, poultry, and sweets.

A steward looked after the servants and money needed to run the castle's household. A bailiff made sure the serfs and farmers who lived on the lord's land paid the rents and crops they owed. Grooms trained the horses that were the pride of the lord and his knights. Many lords also had a falconer to take care of the hawks and falcons used for hunting.

Young knights in training—who were 7 to about 18 years old—also lived in the castle of a wealthy lord, along with troops of foot soldiers. Foot soldiers, who owned no horses, were far less respected than knights, and they were the first to be sent into battle to defend their lord.

When visitors arrived in a castle's courtyard, everyone who lived within the castle walls would turn out to welcome them. A lord and his family usually traveled in a large group that included knights and servants.

13

UNDER THE CASTLE'S SHADOW

he castle promised safety, and villages were built around its walls on the lord's land. The village families each lived in a drafty one-room hut. These small, humble homes had walls made of timber and a thick mixture of mud, straw, and animal hair. The roof was made of thatched straw, and the floor was packed, cold earth.

In the center of the room a cooking fire smoked and crackled, giving off the only heat in winter. There was no chimney, so smoke escaped through a hole in the roof or a windowlike hole in a wall.

The huts were built in a circle, around an open area called the "village green." Each village usually had a church and a mill. Three big fields and stretches of forest land, owned by the lord, surrounded the village. Every year the villagers used one field to grow barley and one to grow another grain, such as wheat or rye. Nothing was planted on the last field so that the soil could rest.

Most of the crops raised by the villagers went into the castle's storehouses. The villagers also paid the lord with goods such as honey from their beehives and chickens that they raised on the tiny lots around their huts. Deer, wild boar, and other game roamed the lord's forests, but the villagers were not allowed to hunt there for food.

Most villagers worked as farmers, but a few learned skills as blacksmiths, carpenters, and shoemakers. Such craftspeople also owed rent and work to the lord.

Whether farmers or craftspeople, serfs or free men and women, the villagers worked from dawn to dusk. Still, there were days set aside for fun and rest. At Christmas the villagers visited the castle for a great feast. Each spring there was a merry fair, and acrobats, jugglers, and musicians performed on the village green. Everyone danced and played games, enjoying a well-earned holiday.

Villagers lived in one-room huts made from wood, mud, and straw. Most villagers were farmers, but some practiced crafts such as carpentry and shoemaking.

RAISING THE CASTLE WALLS

astles towered above everything else on the landscape. They were often built on top of steep hills or above rocky harbors, which made them hard to reach, especially by an enemy. From this high ground, castle guards could see enemy soldiers who were many miles away.

Castle builders trained for many years and traveled throughout Europe to build the castles of great lords. These skilled workers, known as "master craftsmen," included engineers, stonemasons, mortar makers, carpenters, and plumbers.

Master craftsmen watched over the work of hundreds of ordinary men and women who lived near the castle site.

Castle builders used scaffolding, ramps, pulleys, and other devices to lift the heavy stones and fit them into place in castle walls.

Sometimes, if a lord had a great deal of money or a war to be fought, castles could be built within a few years. More often, the building took a lifetime. The lord's family lived in one part of the castle while work went on in another.

For a while, castles were built from strong timber. But wood could be burned in an attack. So new cutting tools and lifting devices were created that made stone castles possible. Builders set up wooden scaffolding and ramps against the sides of castles under construction. Then they raised the walls, stone by stone, toward the sky.

Great lords were rich enough to build huge stone castles. Less wealthy lords continued to build small timber castles. As many as 10,000 castles were built in Germany alone during the Middle Ages. While wood castles did not last, thousands of stone castles still stand today. They can be seen in Great Britain, France, Germany, Spain, and other European countries.

DRAWBRIDGES AND TOWERS

o two castles looked exactly the same, but many had a similar design. Friends and foes alike approached the castle across a cleared "no-man's-land." Surrounding the castle were outer walls called "curtain walls." In a large castle these could be as high as 30 feet, as thick as 20 feet, and as much as 650 feet around (more than double the length of a football field). On top of the curtain walls ran a broad walkway, shielded from the outside world by a stone parapet. Deep gaps in the parapet allowed defenders of the castle to shoot arrows at enemies below.

If an enemy climbed over the curtain walls, the castle's defenders could retreat into the towers at each corner of the walls. The towers had no windows, only slits called "murder holes" that were just wide enough to shoot an arrow through.

Visitors to the castle faced a deep moat filled with water. The moat could be crossed only by traveling over a drawbridge lowered from the far side. Creatures like crocodiles and legendary dragons did *not* live in moats. But the moat's muddy, dirty water was still an effective barrier to unwanted visitors.

Once across the moat, visitors faced a heavy iron gate called a "portcullis." Next they traveled through a series of courtyards, called "baileys," each with its own set of walls and towers. A small castle might have only a single bailey. The outer baileys of large castles held workers' huts, stables, storerooms for food and wine, a bakery, a laundry, and gardens. Only when visitors reached the inner bailey had they at last reached the heart of the castle.

At the inner bailey was a castle's keep, its most important structure. The keep, also known as the "donjon," was a fortified tower. In a small castle, the keep might reach 30 feet—the height of a 3-story building. In a large castle, it might loom higher than 200 feet, or 20 stories. This was the place where the knights of the castle would retreat if the entire castle was overrun by the enemy. Deep in the keep's basement lay dungeons for prisoners and emergency storerooms for food.

Near the keep was the great hall, where the nobles who lived in the castle and their guests dined and spent leisure time. In the earliest castles, the lord's family, knights, and household servants all slept in the great hall. Later, other rooms were added, such as bedrooms, nurseries, offices, and even a little chapel.

A castle made of wood

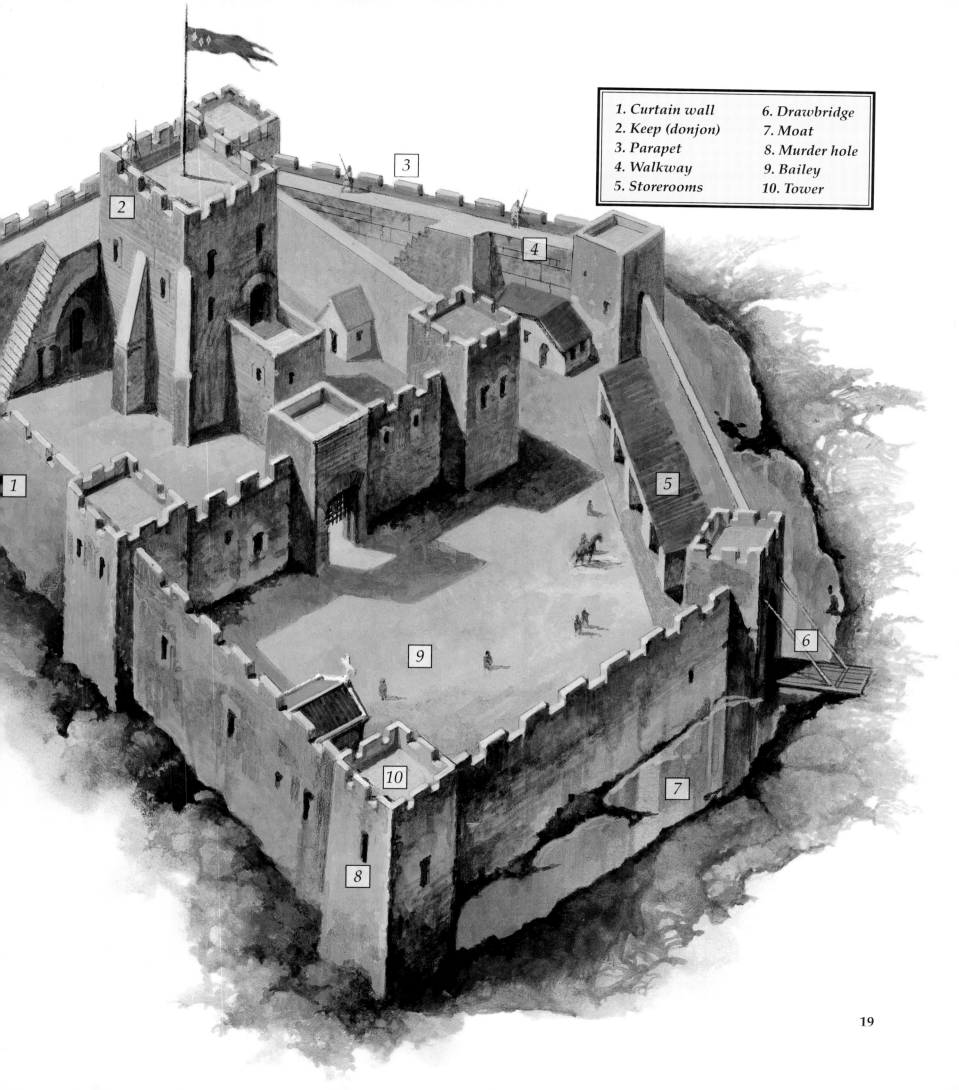

1. Curtain wall
2. Keep (donjon)
3. Parapet
4. Walkway
5. Storerooms
6. Drawbridge
7. Moat
8. Murder hole
9. Bailey
10. Tower

19

DUNGEONS

very castle, no matter how large or small, had its dungeons. Sometimes these dark, stuffy rooms were only a few feet below the great hall. Through tiny air holes, prisoners might hear music and the voices of their captors. Dungeons were also filthy holes in the depths of the keep, where water dripped down the walls, and rats crawled across the floor.

Knights and lords captured in war were usually given enough food and kept in a part of the castle that was sparsely furnished but not totally uncomfortable. There they waited for their lord or family to pay a ransom of gold, armor, or jewels for their freedom. But ordinary men and women were not treated as well. For real or suspected crimes, they could be stripped naked, thrown into a dungeon, and forgotten for years.

Anyone—whether a wealthy knight or a lowly bandit—accused of a serious crime, such as robbery, murder, or treason, could be tortured. Torture was used to obtain a prisoner's confession and get information about others who had taken part in the wrongdoing. In some dungeons, prisoners could be hung upside down from a ring in the ceiling. Some dungeons had an iron chair that was moved close to a blazing fire and became unbearably hot to sit in. Others had a device with a screw that could be tightened to squeeze the thumb of the prisoner.

In the Middle Ages most people accused of a serious crime were treated in a cruel and brutal way. Out of those centuries, however, came one important tradition. Unlike a villager, a lord or nobleman accused of a crime could not be imprisoned forever. He was eventually given a trial before a group of other lords, called a "jury of his peers," or equals. Today, in democratic countries, anyone accused of a crime has the right to a fair trial, which is heard either by a judge or by a judge and jury.

In the Middle Ages, punishment for prisoners was harsh and cruel. Some were starved, whipped, or even hung upside down from a ring in the dungeon's ceiling.

DEFENDING THE CASTLE

hroughout the Middle Ages, warfare was a way of life for lords and knights. They fought one another for land, for possessions, and even over minor insults. Feuding lords often expected an attack upon their castle and were ready for battle. But sometimes enemies attacked by surprise.

Castle guards, high on the curtain walls, were the first to see an enemy's army approaching across the open countryside. They sounded an alarm, and all those within the castle prepared for battle. The villagers fled into the castle for safety. The gate to the courtyard slammed shut and the drawbridge was raised.

When the attack began, the foot soldiers sprang into action first. From behind the parapet they shot thousands of arrows. From the top of the curtain walls they poured streams of boiling oil. Meantime the enemy's foot soldiers continued to attack, pounding the castle walls with battering rams. They filled in the moat with earth or dug tunnels beneath it in order to cross to the castle. Then they hauled huge siege engines up to the walls, and they shot arrows into the outer bailey. Using a catapult—a 40-ton slingshot—they hurled rocks and 60-pound boulders a distance of 500 feet, almost twice the length of a football field.

As soon as an enemy actually climbed the castle walls, knights joined foot soldiers in hand-to-hand combat. Courtyard by courtyard, room by room, knights fought one another with sword and dagger, struggling for control of the castle. Many knights and foot soldiers on both sides died in the bloody combat. Defeated and wounded knights were held by the victor for a ransom of money, armor, or jewels.

Yet it was extremely difficult for even the strongest enemy to capture a castle. A group of 60 knights and foot soldiers could defend the castle against 10 times as many attackers. A siege sometimes went on for months or even years. If nothing else succeeded, the enemy tried to starve the castle's inhabitants by stopping all food supplies. Usually the castle's storerooms held at least two years' worth of food.

To attack a castle, invading armies used catapults that hurled huge boulders over the castle walls.

CASTLE COMFORTS

I n the early Middle Ages, castles were not very comfortable places in which to live. Small, high windows, covered with oiled cloth, allowed little light into the rooms. Candles made of wax and animal fat shed a golden glow, but they smelled badly. During the summer the castle was hot. During the winter a blazing fire in the center of the great hall made clouds of smoke and left the corners of the room chilly. Only shields and lances hung on the walls. There was little furniture. In fact, until the 1100s everyone—from the lord to his most humble servant—slept on the floor, with a thin straw mat for a bed.

During the 1100s castles became more comfortable and even luxurious. Beautifully embroidered tapestries and banners that displayed the lord's coat of arms decorated the larger rooms. By the end of the Middle Ages, murals of hunting scenes or stories from the Bible covered walls and ceilings, and light shone through windows of richly colored glass.

The lord and his lady started to sleep in their own bedroom. It held a big wooden bed with a cozy feather mattress and a handsome chest for clothes. Other important members of the household also received their own bedrooms.

Fashions changed as well. During peaceful times wealthy lords favored silk, velvet, and brocade tunics over the wool or linen ones they wore in battle. Since clothing had no pockets, men carried purses belted to their waists. Ladies dressed in brightly colored gowns, which they kept for a lifetime. Sometimes they also wore large headdresses. Buttons did not exist in Europe until the 1200s, so until then people either tied their clothes or fastened them with jeweled pins.

Members of a castle's household—a lord and lady, knights, noblewomen, and any guests—gathered in the great hall for conversation and entertainment, such as reading or listening to music.

THE DAILY LIVES OF NOBLES AND THEIR CHILDREN

 nobleman had many responsibilities and many roles to play in his daily life. He was a warrior, a landlord, and a judge. Poor villagers asked his permission to postpone their rent, or a widow asked his consent to remarry.

The lord also settled arguments between people who lived on his land, and he ordered punishments for crimes. There were fines for minor offenses, but a villager convicted of a serious crime, such as hunting in the lord's forests, could be hanged or have one of his hands cut off.

Since lords often rode away to war, their wives had to be ready and able to take over all the household responsibilities. Ladies also handled the finances of the castle and managed the staff of servants.

A lord often settled arguments between people who lived on his land. For example, when one person accused another of stealing, the lord heard both sides of the story, then decided who was right and what the punishment should be for the wrongdoer.

The daughters of a lord and lady learned arts such as spinning, sewing, and music. Their sons were educated either to become priests in the Church or to become knights. Sometimes the son of a lord or knight was sent away to the castle of a greater lord for his education.

In their spare time, lords and knights took part in competitive sports, such as fencing, which allowed them to practice their skills. Everyone in the castle, including the lady and her daughters, enjoyed activities such as hunting and games such as chess and backgammon.

A NOBLE FEAST

he great hall glows with the flickering light of candles and torches. Delicious smells of roasted meats and tasty stews fill the air. Lively music from lutes and harps echoes in the huge stone hall, along with the many happy voices of those who have gathered to share the night's feast.

The lord, his lady, and their honored guests sit at a high table, called the "dais." Other visitors and members of the household sit at long tables arranged at right angles to the dais.

Only the lord and lady of the castle have their own plates and cups. Everyone else shares—a cup and plate are set between every two people. Young pages hurry to and fro, serving the meal. Forks are rare, so everyone uses knives, spoons, and fingers. To make eating easier, carvers cut the roasts into small chunks that can be chewed from the end of a knife.

The diners feast on course after course of pork, pheasant, swan, peacock, meat from deer called "venison," and other game from the lord's forests. They toss the leftovers and bones to the hungry hounds beside the table. The diners wash down their meal with huge goblets of ale or wine. For dessert there are pastries, custards, and cakes. In a balcony above the hall, minstrels sing and play all night long. They entertain their listeners with love songs and ballads.

Such dinners were not unusual at the castles of great lords in the Middle Ages. In fact, feasts became even grander on special holidays such as Easter and Christmas. Cooks took pride in creating very fancy holiday dishes. Peacocks were served whole, with their feathers spread. Pies were filled with live birds that flew out when the pastry was cut. Using sugar and jelly, cooks molded huge desserts in the shapes of castles or churches.

A feast in the great hall would last for many hours. While a lord and lady and their guests enjoyed a plentiful meal, they were entertained by musicians, acrobats, and jesters.

30

THE ART OF THE HUNT

t's daybreak. The countryside around the castle is quiet and still. Suddenly the sharp blast of a horn signals the start of a hunt. Armed with nets, spears, and bows and arrows, lords and knights gallop on their horses across meadows and woods, chasing down a wild boar.

Swift greyhounds and foxhounds race ahead, catching the scent of their prey. At last the dogs corner the angry boar in a sunny clearing, and they howl to alert the hunters.

Afterward the hounds will be rewarded with a taste of the freshly killed boar. The rest will be served as a roast or in a pie at the next day's dinner.

Hunters of the Middle Ages also captured smaller prey using trained hawks and falcons. These rare birds came from as far north as Iceland and were even more difficult to train than hunting dogs. The chief falconer, who took care of them, was an important member of the castle's staff.

Knights and noblewomen hunted with hawks. This favorite sport was called hawking.

Hawks and falcons often wore little bells on their legs to identify them. Tiny hoods prevented them from seeing and becoming excited by the activities around them. Each hawk was attached to one gloved wrist of its owner by a silver chain. When a flurry of wild quails, partridges, or pheasants flew into the sky, the owner released the hawk, snatching off its hood. The hawk flew up into the sky, then swooped down for the kill. Then, with its little bell ringing, it returned to its owner.

Many lords and ladies became so fond of their hawks that they carried the birds on their wrists everywhere—even to feasts at the castle.

33

PAGE AND SQUIRE

I t took many years for boys to learn the skills of knighthood. Boys who were chosen to become knights were often the sons and grandsons of knights. At about age 7, they would be sent to the castle of a powerful lord for training and education.

From age 7 to 14, a young knight in training was called a "page." A page learned how to fence, wrestle, and ride a horse. He was taught how to read and write, and learned manners and music as well. Pages had many duties, including serving dinner in the great hall.

At the age of 14, the page became a squire and was assigned to serve one knight. The squire helped the knight put on his armor, slept on the floor beside his master's bed, and did any kind of work his master asked of him.

The squire continued to sharpen his skills as a warrior, learning how to move in heavy armor and to use a knight's weapons. Lances were very awkward, so the squire practiced by lunging over and over at a dummy called a "quintain."

Squires followed knights into battle but were usually not wounded, since knights thought it was dishonorable to fight them. On the battlefield a squire helped his knight any way he could; if a knight was wounded, a squire often dragged him to safety.

The squire also learned that, as a knight, he should behave correctly at all times. A knight was supposed to act with mercy as well as courage on the battlefield. Off the battlefield the squire had to learn how to be a pleasant and courteous companion to others in the castle household.

Practicing fencing

Practicing horsemanship and jousting

Studying music

A knight in training practiced many different skills and performed many duties for his master.

Caring for his master's armor

Sleeping by his master's bed

Serving at meals

DUBBING OF A KNIGHT

or seven years a squire served his master in peace and in war. When he was about 21, a squire who had proved himself brave and loyal was ready to be a knight. Sometimes a squire won knighthood on the battlefield for a brave deed. Usually squires were knighted in the castle during a time of peace.

Only knights could grant knighthood, which they did in a ceremony called "dubbing." At first dubbings were very simple. The squire knelt in front of the parrain, or person knighting him. With his hand or sword the parrain struck a heavy blow on the squire's shoulder, saying, "I dub you knight."

Over the centuries, dubbing grew into a grand ceremony. The day before, the squire bathed in clear water as a symbol that he was washing away his bad deeds. Then he put on a snow-white tunic and a bright red cloak. The white was a sign of his purity. The red stood for his willingness to shed his own blood in battle. Finally he shaved his beard, as a way to show his desire to serve God. He spent the entire night alone in the chapel, thinking and praying.

A crowd of well-wishers attended the ceremony the next morning. The lord and lady were there, as were all the knights of the castle. By the 1200s the parrain's heavy blow had been softened to a gentle tap, but the meaning stayed the same: A knight swore to defend the poor and weak and to wage war against his lord's enemies.

At the end of the ceremony the parrain helped the proud young man put on his glittering new armor. A razor-sharp sword was strapped to his side, and shiny spurs were fastened to his heels. The new knight immediately raced outside and, showing off his skill and strength, leapt onto his horse's back. Glorious adventures now awaited him.

In a ceremony called "dubbing," a squire was touched on his shoulder with a sword as the person knighting him proclaimed, "I dub you knight."

THE CODE OF CHIVALRY

 true knight loyally served his lord and his king. He helped the poor and weak. He behaved bravely in battle. He followed the laws of God, set down by the Church. These ideas about a true knight's behavior became known as the "code of chivalry." The code of chivalry, which came about in the late 1000s, gave knights a higher purpose. Knights became more than rough bullies who cared only about fighting and gaining wealth. Some knights, called "knights errant," traveled from place to place and defended anyone who needed protection, or they joined other knights to fight for a good cause.

By the late 1100s another knightly tradition had developed, called "courtly love," and it also became part of the code of chivalry. This tradition glorified the romantic love between a knight and a lady. To please the woman who had won his heart, a chivalrous knight learned to be courteous and gentle. He composed poems and love songs for her. Sometimes a knight acted bravely in the name of his beloved. And sometimes he did something foolish. For example, one knight refused to sleep in a bed until the lady of his choice told him she loved him. Another courted a lady for ten years—before she even agreed to talk to him.

The centuries between the 1000s and the 1400s have been called the Golden Age of Chivalry. Many of our ideas about loyalty, bravery, helping the weak, and romance have come from this long-ago age.

A French queen named Eleanor of Aquitaine helped the tradition of courtly love to grow. At her castle in France in the 1100s, she created an actual "court of love." Knights and ladies came to the court from far and wide to have their romantic questions and quarrels settled by Eleanor's "judges." Had a certain knight been brave enough to prove his love? Had a certain lady behaved too cruelly to deserve the affection of her handsome suitor?

A chivalrous knight wrote poems, sang songs, and performed brave deeds to please the noblewoman who had won his heart.

TOURNAMENTS

hen a lord decided to hold a tournament, he sent messengers across the countryside to announce it. Knights from far and wide came to compete and show off their skills. Tournaments, which were like mock battles, were usually held at a large field near the castle. The lord and lady and many guests and visitors watched the matches from galleries, which were raised platforms with seats, much like modern-day bleachers.

40

With a fanfare of trumpets, heralds announced the names of the knights who were about to face each other in a jousting match. Spectators in the galleries leaned forward excitedly. Bright red, gold, purple, and silver banners draped the galleries and fluttered in the breeze.

A hush fell over the crowd as the two contestants, wearing glittering armor, emerged from the gates at either end of the field. Riding their huge horses, or chargers, the men cantered toward each other. They lowered their weapons, and a loud clash of lances and shields filled the air. The chargers whirled and turned; the two knights met again and again, each determined to unseat the other. The winner of the match received the loser's horse and armor. If the loser wanted them back, he had to pay for them with gold.

In early tournaments, knights took part in wild contests called "melees." Hundreds of men galloped against one another at the same time, just as in a real battle. So many knights were killed or wounded in these free-for-all fights that new rules had to be invented.

In later tournaments that featured jousts, the ends of a knight's weapons had to be blunted. Still, knights could cause serious wounds in a joust. Tournaments grew even more important toward the end of the Middle Ages, when real battles were less frequent.

Tournaments gradually became magnificent festivals, with jousts, feasts, and entertainment that went on for days. Visiting knights stayed in colorful tents on the castle grounds. Each evening, after the jousts had ended, knights and ladies feasted and danced until after midnight.

As spectators watched from galleries, knights on horseback charged at each other and fought with lances during a jousting match.

LEGENDS OF MANY LANDS

Knights did not always live by the code of chivalry. Just like people today, there were good knights and bad knights, wise knights and foolish knights.

Some knights behaved politely toward wealthy women but unkindly toward the wives and daughters of poor workers. Many knights fought for no other reason than greed. Knights could be bloodthirsty killers. One knight alone, Sir Bevis of Hampton, slaughtered close to 700 people in the many battles he waged during his lifetime.

Still, the singers and poets of the Golden Age of Chivalry composed glorious songs about courageous heroes. These songs and poems told stories that entertained and also taught lessons about bravery. Often the deeds of actual men from the past inspired the tales. For example, the brave act of a warrior who served Charlemagne, the king of the Franks in the late 700s, was told in *The Song of Roland*, which was first sung in the 1100s. The story of a Spanish knight named Rodrigo Díaz de Vivar, who lived in the 1000s, was told in *The Poem of the Cid*, which was first written in 1140.

Since few people knew how to read or write, these stories were learned by memory and often sung. They were told again and again, a little differently by each storyteller. As a result, the stories differed from the facts in several ways. First, in the stories the heroes behaved more like chivalrous knights of the 1100s than real warriors of earlier times, who were rougher and less educated.

Second, the legends also became more exaggerated with each telling. They described how the heroes fought monsters and dragons, rescued beautiful ladies, and saved whole kingdoms from destruction.

The knights of the Golden Age of Chivalry grew up listening to these stories and were inspired by them. The finest real-life knights of Europe during the Middle Ages tried to model themselves on legendary heroes of the past.

Legends of brave knights who battled dragons and other fierce, imaginary monsters were favorite stories of the Middle Ages.

KING ARTHUR AND HIS KNIGHTS

he story of King Arthur and the Knights of the Round Table was a favorite legend of the late Middle Ages. Today it is the best-known and best-loved story of the time. This classic tale may have been based on the life and battles of a great leader who lived in Britain in the 500s. But no one knows this leader's name for sure.

King Arthur and his knights sat at the Round Table to show that they were all equal.

The story begins when Arthur was a boy and many lords were at war for the crown of Britain. Young Arthur had been taken in by a kind knight and was living happily in the knight's castle. Only a wise old magician named Merlin knew anything about Arthur's true background—or his destiny.

One day, Arthur followed his foster brother, Kay, to a tournament. Kay had forgotten his sword and told Arthur to go back to the castle to get it. On the way, Arthur saw a sword stuck deep in a stone. After lifting the sword out, he returned to the tournament, where he gave the rusty weapon to Kay.

Kay looked down at the sword and could not believe what he saw. Other knights gathered around Kay and Arthur. They, too, were amazed. None of the proud knights had ever been able to pull the mysterious sword from the stone. The knights read the words written on the sword and suddenly knelt before Arthur. On the sword it said: *He who pulls this sword from the stone is the rightful king of Britain.* Young Arthur was none other than the lost son of Britain's last ruler.

The legend says that as king of Britain, Arthur made the land peaceful and drove away invaders. He built a great castle at Camelot, where the bravest knights in the land came to live. The knights sat at the Round Table—a table that had no special seat of honor. This showed that the knights were all equal and at peace with one another. From Camelot they rode forth to do good deeds and to battle dragons and other enemies.

Many of Arthur's knights took part in the search for the Holy Grail, the cup from which Jesus drank at the Last Supper. It was said that the Holy Grail had the power to help the troubled people of the world. But it had been lost for many centuries. It was believed that only someone pure in heart could find this holy treasure. Arthur's knight Sir Galahad succeeded in the quest, but the Grail later vanished.

After young Arthur pulled the sword from the stone, he became king of Britain.

King Arthur built a magnificent castle at Camelot.

Sir Galahad found the highly treasured Holy Grail.

THE CONQUEST OF ENGLAND

n 1066 an army from Normandy invaded the island of Great Britain. It sailed across the English Channel, its boats filled with battle-ready soldiers, knights, and horses.

At that time many of the present countries of Europe were divided into small kingdoms. Most were not the same nations that you see on a map today. Normandy, located in what is now France, was a separate state. The lord who ruled Normandy, named William, held as much power as a king.

Under the command of William of Normandy, later known as William the Conqueror, the Normans attacked the Saxon army of King Harold, the ruler of England. England was, as it still is, the largest country on the island of Great Britain. This bloody struggle between Normans and Saxons became known as the Battle of Hastings.

46

King Harold was already weary from fighting other rivals who had challenged his rule. Still, the armies of the Normans and the Saxons seemed evenly matched. Both armies had about 5,000 men, all armed with swords and lances. However, 2,000 Norman soldiers were mounted on horseback. The Saxons fought on foot. The horsemen made a big difference, for the Normans had the advantage of their animals' speed, force, and height.

The Normans won the Battle of Hastings, and their victory changed England forever. It gave England a new ruler, William, who united the land under a stronger government than ever before. William brought many Norman lords with him. He rewarded them with land and castles in England and made the defeated Saxons serfs.

The Norman Conquest began the age of feudalism and knighthood in England, where it would last for many centuries.

William of Normandy sailed his army over the English Channel to invade England.

THE CRUSADES

n the early Middle Ages the city of Jerusalem was ruled by Muslims who permitted Christian travelers from Europe to come and go. Deeply religious Christians called "pilgrims" made the long and dangerous trip to Jerusalem to visit holy shrines and temples. They walked for thousands of miles and then crossed the Mediterranean Sea in rickety, leaky boats.

In the 1000s new Muslim leaders conquered Jerusalem. Unlike the early rulers, they closed the city to outsiders. The Christian population of Europe was outraged. The Pope, the head of the Church, called upon the knights of Europe to fight a holy war, or Crusade, against the Muslims. The Pope hoped a Crusade would reopen Jerusalem to Christians. He also hoped a Crusade far away in Jerusalem would keep the knights from fighting among themselves at home.

The Crusaders' journey to Jerusalem was long and hard, covering thousands of miles. But crusading knights and ordinary people alike made the trip in order to defend their religious beliefs.

A crusading knight wore a white tunic with a red cross.

A Muslim warrior fought with a long, curved sword and a pike.

Knights everywhere wanted to join the First Crusade, which began in 1095. Thousands of knights and ordinary people, shouting the battle cry "God Wills It," made the long trip over land and sea. Many died from sickness or lack of food. Others froze to death or drowned. The knights of the First Crusade conquered Jerusalem, but the city was soon recaptured by Muslims. Over the next 200 years, there were eight more Crusades.

A knight on a Crusade could be recognized easily, for he wore a white tunic with a bright red cross sewn on it. The word *Crusade* comes from a Latin word meaning "cross." Many knights went on the Crusades because of their religious beliefs. Others went simply for adventure or to gain wealth.

The Children's Crusade took place in 1212. Thousands of boys and girls between the ages of 10 and 18 began the journey to Jerusalem. The children believed that their strong religious faith and goodness would give them the power to win back the city. But few survived to reach the Holy Land.

The Crusades changed life in Europe in many ways. The European people who traveled to the Middle East brought back goods to trade, such as spices and silk. But, even more important, they brought back new ideas and knowledge about art and science.

Led by the Black Prince, English foot soldiers used longbows and steel-tipped arrows to defeat French knights during the Hundred Years' War.

THE HUNDRED YEARS' WAR

terrible war between France and England broke out in the mid-1300s and lasted for over 100 years. The war began because Edward III, king of England, believed he had a claim to the throne of France.

At first it looked as though the English forces had little chance of winning. In France, at the Battle of Crécy, English foot soldiers faced the bravest French knights on horseback. But this did not worry the English commander. He was King Edward's son, known as the Black Prince because he wore shiny black armor.

Under the Black Prince's leadership, the English foot soldiers fought magnificently, using a new weapon called the "longbow." The English killed a thousand French knights with their steel-tipped arrows. The French forces could not recover. Their best knights had been slain. The Battle of Crécy marked the first time foot soldiers had defeated knights.

For years, long after the Black Prince had died, the battles continued. Then, in the mid-1400s, an amazing event took place. A teenage French country girl named Joan of Arc declared she had heard the voices of three saints. Joan said the voices told her to go to the aid of the prince of France, known as the "Dauphin." Joan went to the highest commanders of the French army and convinced them to let her help. Finally, with the Dauphin's permission, the army commanders gave her armor, a horse, and a lance. Joan rode at the front of the French forces and led them to a series of astonishing victories over the English.

In 1430 Joan of Arc was captured, and she was put to death in 1431. But Joan's faith and leadership were always remembered by the French army. The French continued to win victory after victory, finally driving the English out of France.

THE CASTLE'S DECLINE

By the 1400s the lives of nobles as well as of ordinary people were changing. The Crusaders had brought back knowledge from other lands. New inventions, such as the printing press, helped to spread this knowledge.

Before the printing press, books had to be copied by hand, one at a time. Books were very rare because they were so difficult to make. Now many copies of books could be printed, spreading knowledge more widely than ever before. More and more people learned how to read and write.

In the cities of Italy, an age called the "Renaissance" had already begun. The word *Renaissance* means "rebirth." During this time important knowledge that had been forgotten for hundreds of years was rediscovered. People took a new interest in science, mathematics, art, literature, and learning of all kinds.

One invention from the Far East ended the age of knights and castles. Gunpowder, which was invented in China, was first used in Europe in the mid-1300s. At first soldiers did not know how to handle it. They wounded themselves more often than their enemies.

But during the 1400s soldiers learned to fire cannons and guns. Cannonballs easily burst holes in stone castle walls that had stood up to every other kind of weapon. Castles crumbled under such attacks and could no longer protect those inside from their enemies. By the 1500s, instead of building fortlike stone castles, most lords and ladies lived in elegant palaces or comfortable country homes.

Gunpowder also weakened the role of the knight. Weapons like muskets, when fired from a distance, could kill a knight wearing the heaviest armor. Artillerymen, who were paid to fight, soon became more valuable to kings than their most loyal knights.

Once gunpowder and firearms came into use, castles were no longer useful for protection. Their thick stone walls crumbled when hit by cannonballs.

A CHANGING WORLD

Born in France in 1476, Pierre Bayard was one of the last true knights. By this time most soldiers were paid for their work. They no longer owed loyalty to a lord or tried to obey the strict code of chivalry. But Pierre was different. As a boy, he loved to hear stories about the knights in his family's history, almost as much as those about King Arthur. Pierre wanted to be a knight and practiced jousting, fencing, and riding every day. When he turned 18, he got his wish. He was dubbed a knight and set off on horseback to find adventure.

At this time, France was at war with both Spain and Italy. In one battle against the Spanish army, Pierre Bayard defended a bridge single-handedly against 200 Spanish soldiers. In battle after battle, Pierre Bayard became famous throughout Europe, known as the "Chevalier de Bayard, the knight without fear or blame." But all of Pierre Bayard's bravery and skill on the battlefield could not save him from a musket's bullet, which pierced his armor while he fought near the River Sesia in 1524.

Although he was a brave and skilled knight, Pierre Bayard could not defend himself when a bullet pierced his armor.

THE STORY OF DON QUIXOTE

Knighthood had ended in the 1500s, but hundreds of exciting stories were still told about the adventures of men in shining armor. In the 1600s a Spanish author named Miguel de Cervantes set out to write a book that made fun of legends about knights and their brave deeds. The hero of Cervantes's story was an elderly gentleman named Don Quixote.

Don Quixote loved stories about knights so much that he often imagined himself as a great hero in shining armor. His daydreams seemed so real that one day he made a helmet out of cardboard, put on a rusty suit of armor, mounted a skinny old horse, and set off to do good deeds.

The story of his adventures is both funny and sad. When Don Quixote comes upon a windmill, he imagines that it is a fierce giant with long arms. Of course, it is his duty as a true knight to attack the awful "giant," and he does. The "giant" wins the battle, tossing Don Quixote high in the air. Don Quixote has many other adventures. He rarely wins his battles but is always determined to be a brave and chivalrous knight.

A GOLDEN AGE LIVES ON

Today we often read stories about King Arthur and the Knights of the Round Table. We enjoy chess and backgammon—the same games once played by knights of the Middle Ages. Mysterious knights in black armor or gallant knights in gleaming silver are featured in everything from space movies to computer games. And every year thousands of tourists visit the castles of Europe. Many are in ruins, but some are still standing and look as mighty and majestic as they did centuries ago. In democratic countries, such as the United States, people are entitled to trials by their "peers," or equals, just like the lords of feudal Europe. And we continue to value loyalty, courtesy, and courage in the face of danger. These are part of our inheritance from the Middle Ages. They are the same values that the true knight lived by.

The centuries of knights and castles may be over, but their magic still surrounds us.
People of every age can dream about glory, adventure, courage, and heroes in shining armor.
Images of the golden age of knights and castles are seen today in all kinds of
popular entertainment, from comic books and video games to television and films.

INDEX